Is that my cat?

To all the cats I have ever had the pleasure to know,
fat or otherwise.
J.A.

ISBN 978-0-545-83738-5

Text and illustrations copyright © 2014 by Jonathan Allen. All rights reserved.
Published by Scholastic Inc., 557 Broadway, New York, NY 10012,
by arrangement with Boxer Books Limited. SCHOLASTIC and associated logos are
trademarks and/or registered trademarks of Scholastic Inc.

12 11 10 9 8 7 6 5 4 3 2 1   15 16 17 18 19 20/0

Printed in the U.S.A.   40

First Scholastic printing, January 2015

The illustrations were prepared digitally by the author.
The text is set in Bang.

Is that my cat?

Jonathan Allen

SCHOLASTIC INC.

Is that my cat?
It can't be.

My cat is a slim,
sleek kitty cat.

Is that my cat?
It can't be.

My cat *is* a little cat who leaps in and out of the cat flap.

Is this my cat?
What happened to the
light little cat I could
pick up with one hand?

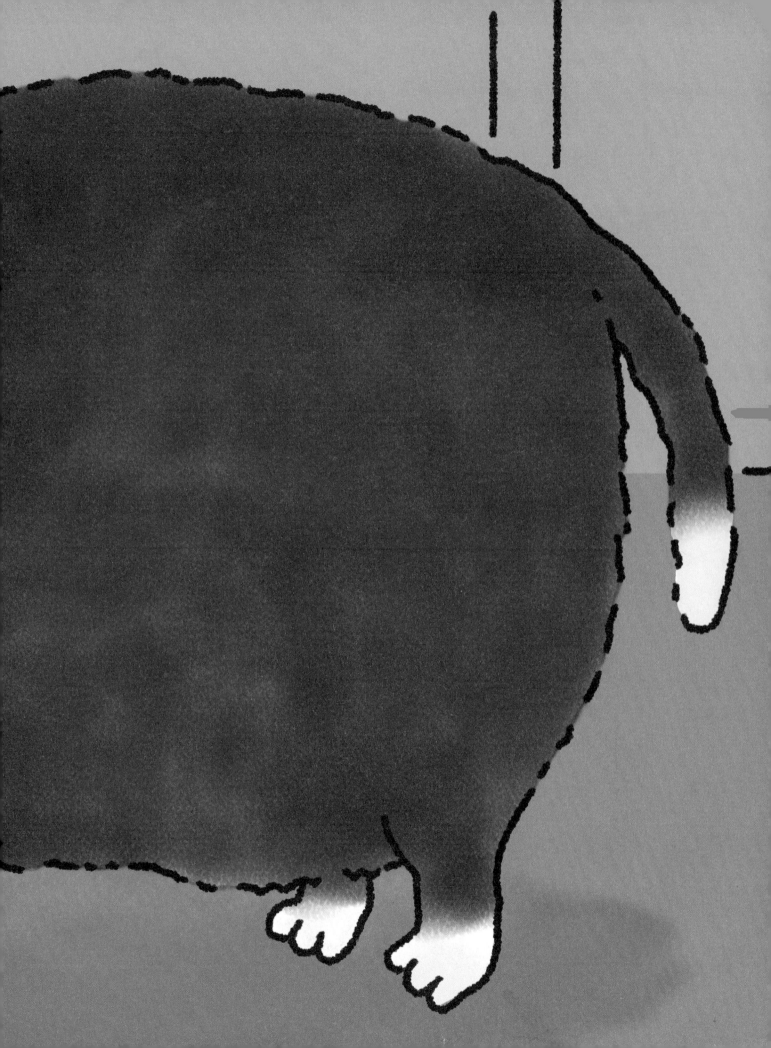

Is that my cat?
No way!
My cat is a mighty
mouse catcher.

Is that my cat?
It can't be.

My cat is a playful puss,
always ready for a game.

That cannot
be my cat.
My cat is a
brave tree
climber.

Is that my cat?
It can't be.
My cat is a wide-awake
cat who sits on the
window sill.

Is that my cat
purring in the
hall closet?

IT IS MY CAT,
and she has kittens.

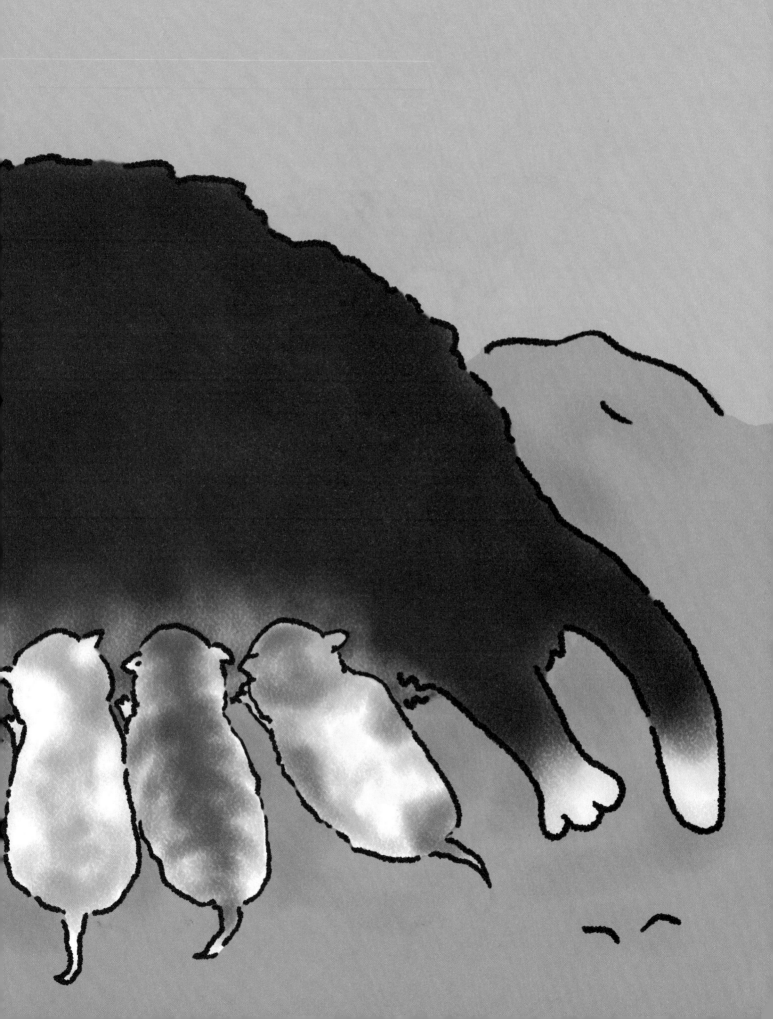

Are they my cats?